Count and Pl K Dot

The Little-Bitty Learning Ladybug

Learning Numbers 1-10 is More Fun with a Friend!

KIMBERLY BECKER

"Hi, I'm K Dot."

"I'm a teeny-tiny, little-whittle, sassy-frassy, bright and brassy, ladybug!"

"What is your name?"

"Do you
want to be friends?"

"How about some fun...

and we play a game?"

"Let's count to ten, and then do it again!"

"Counting numbers is lots of fun."

"Hello, numbers... here we come."

"Hurray, hurray...
it's time to count
and play."

"Let's count together...
even if it's wet weather."

**"Ready, get set...
let's go!"**

1 One

2 Two

"Tie my shoes."

3 Three

4 Four

"Sweep the floor."

5 Five

6 Six

"Jump over sticks."

7 Seven

8 Eight

"Shut the gate."

9 Nine

10 Ten

"Sit on a big fat hen!"

"Counting to ten is so much fun!"

"Come on friend...

let's do it again!"

1 One

2 Two

"Tie my shoes."

3 Three

4 Four

"Sweep the floor."

 **Five**

 **Six**

"Jump over sticks."

7 Seven

8 Eight

"Shut the gate."

9 Nine

10 Ten

"Sit on a big fat hen!"

"Hurray, hurray... we did it again!"

"Our counting game
is so much fun, let's play it...

under the golden sun!"

1 2 One, two, tie my shoes.................

3 Three, four, sweep the floor.........

4 5 Five, six, jump over sticks...........

6 7 Seven, eight, shut the gate...........

8 9 10 Nine, ten, sit on a big fat hen!

**"Counting numbers
is fun to do."**

Enjoy other projects by
KIMBERLY BECKER
@
www.kimberlybeckerauthor.com

**Look for more of the
K Dot Learning Fun
Series**

Available soon!